Eliza R. M. Birdsall

Star-Dust

gathered by Azile

Eliza R. M. Birdsall

Star-Dust
gathered by Azile

ISBN/EAN: 9783337405656

Printed in Europe, USA, Canada, Australia, Japan

Cover: Foto ©Andreas Hilbeck / pixelio.de

More available books at **www.hansebooks.com**

GATHERED BY

AZILE.

"THE true harvest of my daily life is somewhat as intangible and indescribable as the tints of morning and evening. It is *a little star-dust caught*—a segment of the rainbow which I have clutched."

"O ye stars of heaven! bless ye the Lord; praise Him and magnify Him forever."

NEW-YORK:

ANSON D. F. RANDOLPH,

683 BROADWAY.

1860.

CONTENTS.

...

STAR-DUST.

—•••—

STARS.

BRIGHT stars, that are gleaming
  Up in sky so blue,
Ere I fall to dreaming,
  I must peep at you.

As a sudden smiling
  Lights a face of gloom,
So your pleasant shining
  Gilds my little room.

It is just in keeping
  With my thoughts to-night;
I can leave my sleeping
  Rather than your sight.

1

Hidden in your gleaming,
  Trembling in your rays,
Is a deeper meaning
  Than first meets our gaze.

Nightly am I learning,
  From your golden speech,
From your constant burning,
  Truths I long to teach.

Much the heart feels ever,
  Which the lips conceal;
Spirit-converse never
  Can the tongue reveal.

Else what thrilling stories
  Would mine own now sing
Of the mystic glories
  Ye are whispering.

STAR-DUST.

Would I could tell only
  What ye are to me;
I am never lonely
  With such friends as ye.

Would I could send only
  Some stray rays of light
To some heart more lonely
  Than mine own to-night.

Those that whisper ever:
  Lustrous though we are,
We can rival never,
  The bright "MORNING STAR."

Dull our clearest beaming!
  Purest light how dim!
Dark seems all our gleaming
  When compared to Him.

Though our nightly glimmer
   Makes earth's dimness less,
What our feeble shimmer
   To His power to bless?

We but *clay* can lighten;
   He illumes the *soul*;
Darkest minds will brighten
   'Neath His blest control.

Hearts that know but anguish,
   Think not to be sad;
Hopes that long did languish
   Spring up strong and glad

'Neath His blessed shining.
   For his mellow glow
Gives a "silver lining"
   To each cloud of woe.

Ye, who wander weary,
  In a path-way dim ;
Sinful, sick, and weary,
  Turn, oh ! turn to Him !

Ye, who seek for pleasure
  Where no comforts are,
Seek the only treasure—
  The pure *Morning Star.*

Send I this thought only
  From the stars to-night,
Will some heart now lonely
  Catch the ray of light?

Let us all be learning
  Stars shine not for naught ;
Nightly heed their burning.
  Love them as we ought.

Amid my simple praying,
Which much of evil mars,
Breathes o'er *one* fervent saying,
I bless God for the stars.

A STARRY LESSON.

THEE to the stars I send;
　　Gaze on them as they burn;
And tell me, tell me, friend,
　　Canst thou no lesson learn?

Oh! raise thy glance on high;
　　Behold the looks of light
Clear falling from each eye
　　Of star, so silver bright.

I bid thee read within
　　This steady light, and clear,
The lesson taught by Him
　　Who made each shining sphere.

They look this wide earth o'er;
Thus ever—ever thus
They gaze on sea, on shore,
As now they look on us.

The waters earth doth keep,
Not one of all forgot ;
Each lake, and ocean deep,
Doth hold some shining spot.

So when within a lake
Some little star doth look,
It finds its glance doth make
Its image in the brook.

Its beauty is displayed
As well by ripples clear,
As by the deep, blue shade
Of its own native sphere.

Methinks that twinkle bright,
  Betokens grateful glee ;
It trembles with delight,
  Its image *true* to see.

In this pray what are *we*
  But *stars*, though not as bright?
Who if we can but see
  Clear through some eye of light,

Clear through down to the *heart*,
  Whose channel is the *eye ;*
Joy will the glance impart,
  If we can there espy
                    .

Our image perfect made,
  Both understood and known ;
Our feelings all displayed,
  And cared for as its own.
    1*

In this each is a star;
   Now let us gaze and learn
If in aught else we are
   Stars that so brightly burn.

We'll take that self-same star
   That gazed within the brook;
Its glance now spreading far
   Adown the deep to look.

The ocean is not calm;
   Wave over wave doth leap;
Oh! can it safe from harm
   The starry image keep?

The billows rise and swell;
   They dash against the shore.
Oh! who the fate can tell
   Of star that looketh o'er?

STAR-DUST.

With raging foam they rise
  Beneath high Heaven's brow;
O star of yonder skies!
  Where is thine image now?

A few distorted gleams
  Shine o'er the waves afar;
But naught is there that seems
  Like yonder beaming star.

And could none gaze above,
  But on the deep to see
How stars look down in love,
  Oh! how deceived we'd be!

We'd whisper by the tide:
  Gleams, tell us what ye are;
But restless waves would hide
  The image of the star.

Thus causing asking mind
    An impress wrong to hold,
Like false tale leaves behind
    A stain of whom 'tis told.

How looketh that star now?
    Broken its image lies!
Yet with a calm, pure brow,
    It beams in yonder skies.

Yes, it as bright and still
    Looks on the ocean deep,
As on the little rill
    That doth its likeness keep.

'Tis true the star may mourn,
    The ocean's sin deplore.
But still it gazes on
    High, holy as before!

Can we no lesson learn?
   In this are we stars too?
When we can thus discern
   Ourselves pictured untrue?

Do *we* gaze still the same,
   Perchance with look of scorn,
Disdaining to draw nigh
   And say 'tis falsely drawn?

Disdaining words to hold,
   Or aught of vengeance take
On those who with false mold
   Seek impress wrong to make?

When waves of malice leap,
   And foam with slander's tongue,
And we see in the deep
   Our broken image flung—

Do *we* gaze still the same
　　On raging seas below,
That wildly "foam their shame,"
　　And scarce can harm us so?

For *waves* can't reach a *star!*
　　Nor have they power to take
Its image from, or mar
　　Its shining in the lake.

Go, be a *Star*, my friend,
　　Nor thus of vengeance speak.
And let thy light descend,
　　Of *pardon* pure and meek.

Thy self-respect retain,
　　Whate'er thy foes may do.
The *deed* thy scorn should gain,
　　The *doer*, pity true.

Oh! should a planet fair,
    When thus it sees its wrong,
Dart gleams of angry glare,
    Beaming with vengeance strong;

Or seek to leave its place
    To scorch the unkind wave,
No longer could we trace
    A *star*, but *Passion's slave!*

The picture in the sea
    Then would not be untrue;
No longer would there be
    A holy star to view;

But broken gleams indeed!
    A scattered, fitful light,
From its calm beauty freed,
    And lowered from its hight.

Go, be a star, my friend;
   Shine holy, high, and calm:
If vengeance must descend,
   Oh! let the stronger arm

Of Him who made the sea,
   And the bright stars to shine,
The just avenger be;
   His arm, and *never* thine!

God, beneath the star-light, nightly,
   Help us all to pray arightly;
Father, make us STARS *to be*
Shining evermore for THEE.

WAS IT A DREAM?

A FEELING of weariness had crept into my heart,
and I stole from the midst of gathered friends, into
the garden. The sun had set cloudlessly, and I
knew the night was clear. I longed to look up at
the bright stars, and to have them speak to me;
their language was dearer and more soothing to my
spirit than the merry jests and sportive words of
the gay and light-hearted ones within. The stars
have ever been my most *intimate friends;* from a
little child they have comforted me when sad, and
taught me many a beautiful lesson. When yearning for sympathy, realizing how impossible it is for
dearest earthly friends perfectly to comprehend one
another; when oppressed with an intense feeling
that I longed to share with some one, but could not;

that I longed to utter, but knew not how; when I
would look on other people, and wonder if their
calm, tranquil faces, often cold and passive ones,
concealed such a world as I found within myself;
and whether the hearts of grown people beat the
same as those of little children; and if so, how
they lived through it — for I was sure my own
would burst before it grew to womanhood; then
I would seek the stars, and hold communion with
them; in the interchange of sympathy, most eloquent and tender, I would be subdued; beneath
their lofty calmness I, too, would grow calm. Do
you call this a childish fancy? Then I pity
you, for it is truth. I pity any one who has
not yet found that the great heart of Nature
beats responsively to his. I believe in the deepest
and most perfect communion with every thing
that our Father has made. You may call them

instruments, if you will, upon which He plays
most skillfully; it is His voice which speaks from
the trees, the flowers, the birds, and the stars. His
spirit pervades all; thus every thing in nature be-
comes a channel of communication between earth
and heaven. The stars are the *golden speaking-trum-*
pets through which our Father utters many a word
of blessing and comfort; many a beautiful, glorious
truth, which our *spirits* hear, understand, and reply
to, but which our *tongues* can never speak.

As I said, in my weariness I sought the garden,
to be again soothed and comforted by the stars; but
to my surprise and grief, not one was visible.
What could it mean? The sky was clear, no dark
cloud threatened a storm; no mist or vapor floated
through the atmosphere, to obscure their light; yet
not one could I discern. Disappointed and deeply
grieved, I turned to the flowers, to whisper awhile

with them. But their heads were bowed, their petals shriveled, their green leaves were curled, and so crisp from excessive dryness, that, as I touched them, they crumbled to pieces. Not a drop of dew had fallen, and the poor, thirsty blossoms were parched and dying. "O Earth! Earth!" I moaned, " what new woe hath befallen thee? The cloud of sin raised by our first parents, had not power to vail the starlight; nor even the blood of Abel, as it dyed thee to red clay, could blight thy flowers. What strange enormity has been committed, that the stars should refuse to gaze on thee, the dews shrink from falling on thee, and thy blossoms wither in dread upon thy bosom?" While thus lamenting, a little star trembled forth; not bright and eloquent, as was its wont, but pale and mute; until, as I passionately addressed it, its gleamings alternately deepened and whitened, as moved by its own heart-throbbings. At length it spoke :

"The heavens were so transparent, the atmosphere so clear, and earth so very beautiful at sunset, that I thought, when I peeped down, our whole golden choir would be out, attired in their most resplendent robes, to light earth's darkened places, and to chant to those to whom we nightly give the call—' *He that hath ears to hear, let him hear.*' And that *I*, such a little star, and so dim when compared to my brilliant sisters, could not be missed among so many. I thought that if I rested this one evening none would know it, none would miss the one small ray that I am only capable of emitting. I knew not, until roused by your voice of lamentation, that all my sister stars had thought and felt the same ; that earth was dark and lonely, and that the strange, mysterious thing, that living, breathing dust, called *man*, who is a greater marvel to us than we can ever be to him, whom we watch over with the angels, often forming a golden stairway, so that they can step from star to star with ease, as they go to minister to that 'clay and a breath.' I knew not that these mysterious objects of our united care and love, had listened in vain for our nightly melody, to soothe them to slumber, or that the wakeful spirits amid them had grown weary of waiting for us to come and sing snatches of the glorious harmony which lifts the listening soul above its clay. I knew not this, and now I mourn that I wandered from my place ; for my ray might have cheered *one* little flower, pierced *one* gloomy spot, attracted *one* spirit, causing it to look up, and think of the One who formed us both. I mourn ! I mourn !"

Just then a drop of dew descended, and as it fell it echoed sorrowfully the lament of the star—" I mourn! I mourn! I questioned, What was I among so many? Who could miss a single dew-drop among the myriads that nightly fall? One tiny blade of grass, I said, was all I had to water; and surely dew enough will be upon the earth to nourish that, even if I tarry here; but I, too, heard your moan of sadness, and I hastened to my little spire of grass; but, behold, I am *too late!* it is *dead!* What account can I give in the morning, when the sun's first ray calls me home to bear tidings of my mission? It is unfulfilled! unfulfilled! I mourn! I mourn!"

Suddenly the stars all glimmered, I heard the dew dropping fast and thick around me, the flowers raised their drooping heads, their leaves uncurled, the fading grass revived, and the fragrance, the star-light, and the dew, chanted around me in a soft, rich chorus:

Maiden, 'neath our golden trembling,
    'Neath the dropping of the dew—
Pardon us for once dissembling,
    So to teach this truth to you.

Not a star has light for *hiding*,
    Howe'er dim that light may be,
If within its place abiding,
    It will shine for *somebody*.

Not one drop of dew is vainly
    Fashioned by its Maker's hand;
He who forms it seeth plainly
    If it keepeth His command.

Thou a little star art, Maiden,
    Very dim amid the rest;
Yet with mission art thou laden,
    As the brightest and the best.

Thou a drop of dew art, Maiden,
 Very fleeting, very small ;
Yet with mission art thou laden,
 As the greatest of them all.

Little star, who art thou cheering
 In the sorrow-darkened earth?
Who is blest by thine appearing ?
 Who rejoices in thy birth ?

Drop of dew, is there *one* flower
 Thou hast soothed or comforted ?
Hast thou used thy little power
 To sustain *one* drooping head ?

Let no time be lost in mourning
 That thou art not something grand ;
What *right* hast thou for *self-scorning*,
 Fashioned thus by God's own hand?
2

What can Sun or Moon be doing
More than any little star,
But God's holy will pursuing,
Finding what their missions are ?

Then be faithful in *thy calling*,
Howe'er lowly it may be ;
For star-shining and dew-falling
Surely will bless *somebody*.

STAR-GLEANINGS.

I.

THE COMMAND.

" Ye are the light of the world."

" Let your light so shine before men, that they, seeing your good works, may glorify your Father which is in Heaven."

How high ! how pure they seem !
  So far beyond all strife !
No fitful, wayward gleam
  Disturbs their calm, still life.

Their steady, constant glow,
  So peaceful and serene,
With what is here below
  Strange contrast forms, I ween.

Oh! can ye know, bright stars,
　Of all that passes here?
Of all the sin that mars
　The life upon this sphere?

And yet, perchance ye know,
　And shine on still the same,
To mitigate our woe—
　To make our pathway plain.

Ye know of all our strife—
　Of all our weariness;
Of all wrought in our life
　Of anguish and distress.

And yet shine on! I deem
　We who are called to be
Lights in this world to gleam,
　A truth can learn from ye.

But we are very weak—
   Not calm and high and pure :
Our dimness, who may speak ?
   Our failings, who endure ?

We can not rise *above*
   To shine upon the earth ;
But in it we must move
   Encompassed by the dearth.

And would *ye* be as bright,
   Brought down to dwell with us?
With sin and its dread blight ?
   Still would your light shine thus ?

And yet ye may have woe
   Like ours, dark and deep ;
Ye your own sorrows know—
   Your own secrets keep.

Likewise its joy and woe;
Both are a mystery deep,
Each Christian heart may know,
Each Christian heart may keep,

And yet the while look round
And see one more forlorn;
In sin so firmly bound,
That others gaze with scorn;

Or shrinking, turn away
With thought of hateful dye,
Which actions oft betray,
"Far holier am I!"

Then burns the "*shining light*,"
As stars that wax not dim
Before a woeful sight,
The Christian looks on him.

His own grief laid aside,
  He looks to soothe and cheer;
To aid, to gently chide,
  To rouse yet banish fear.

He looks, 'mid weariness
  And strife with his own sin,
In ways of holiness
  A brother's soul to win.

Oh! let us this thought keep,
  Won from the stars to-night;
They gaze on darkness deep,
  Nor shrink to give their light.

'Tis this we greatly need:
  A *love* for those *most prone*
To err—and hearts to bleed
  For sorrows *not our own.*

Oh ! more of *sympathy*,
   To guide, and soothe, and bless ;
No " *shining* light" can be
   Without this loveliness.

STAR-GLEANINGS.

II.

THE PROMISE.

" They that turn many to righteousness, shall shine as the stars forever and ever."

AY, calm, and pure, and high are ye,
  Stars beautiful and bright.
But very low and sinful we,
  Yet both are *in the night!*

And while ye shine within the dark,
  Most blessed truths to teach,
So must we yield our glow-worm spark,
  Some darker soul to reach.
        2*

And while ye gaze on all our sin,
  Nor sickened, turn away,
So for the erring, room within
  Our hearts, to love and pray.

If thus the pure *Command* we keep,
  To "let our light so shine,"
The *Promise* we shall surely reap;
  Surely it is *Divine.*

And so, whene'er we gaze above,
  The heavens seem enwrought
In golden characters of love,
  With this one cheering thought.

Not always weak, not always dim,
  Not always sinful we;
The light that now burns low within,
  Shall one day glow like ye!

With these deep yearnings fully met
   That haunt us night and day,
Each deed of wrong, each vain regret,
   And strife all passed away.

The struggles o'er to do and be
   That which we best conceive;
The struggles, *without victory!*
   O'er which our hearts now grieve.

The love made pure which now we keep
   Shut up too closely here;
Dear God! so loving we, yet weak,
   We wound the souls most dear!

Ah! sad were we; ah! sad indeed,
   Were not this promise heard;
But now there is a joy decreed
   For all who know the Word.

For all who watch the feet that stray,
  To win them tenderly
To Him, who said, "I am the Way!"
  "Come, weary ones, to Me!"

A joy! for He the Sun shall give
  The light for which we yearn;
And in His presence we shall *live*,
  Forever brightly burn.

"Shine *as the stars!*" so pure and calm,
  From every evil freed;
Upheld by His Almighty arm,
  Fullness of bliss indeed!

Dear Saviour, so unworthy we
  Of all the new world's bliss,
So weak, we can but cry to thee,
  God help us now in th's!

A STAR-THOUGHT.

A STAR peeped out, 'mid the heavens blue,
And looked on the sea, itself to view ;
But the restless wave, and foaming tide,
The lovely form of the star belied.

I gazed on both, and my spirit grieved,
And murmured low the truth it received.
Saviour, 'tis thus thou lookest on me,
Thou art the star, my heart is the sea.

Thou gazest down, pure, lovely, and bright,
For darkened souls to reflect thy light;
But oh ! what trace of thee can be seen
In this restless, surging, fretted stream ?

'Tis true that a passer-by might know,
From gleamy fragments tossed to and fro,
That light of some kind was shining o'er
The sin-crested waves; but nothing more.

I see in a dream a struggling bark,
Shaken and driven o'er waters dark,
By a tempest fierce; at thought of death
The crew stand, trembling, with failing breath.

Yet 'mid the roar of the wild wind's sweep,
The lashing and din of the raging deep,
'Mid the quick rolling the bark must keep,
Lies One in a calm and peaceful sleep!

But He, whom the tempest could not wake,
Whose slumber no howling storm could break,
Doth stir his limbs and unclose his eye,
At the low sound of a mournful cry.

"Master, we perish! dost thou not care?"
He heard, and answered at once their prayer.
Calmly he slept; as calmly he rose,
And gave to the sea the same repose.

The heaving ocean, like a pure rill,
Displayed clear each ray of—" Peace, be still!"
It held, unbroken, the image bright
Of the Star that gazed in placid light.

Saviour, my heart is that stormy sea:
The gale of sin rises fearfully;
The waves perpetual motion keep,
As swayed beneath its powerful sweep.

It trembles in vain beneath thy light,
To display thine image pure aright;
Behold it lying all broken there;
Speak to me, Saviour! dost thou not care?

Just as thou spake to the stormy sea,
Saviour, I pray thee, so speak to me.
Thou only to sin canst say: *Be still!*
Subdue my heart to thy holy will.

Rebuke and subdue, till shining clear,
Thou wilt be perfectly imaged here;
That all who gaze may be won to love
The beautiful " MORNING STAR" above.

ANOTHER STAR-THOUGHT.

SOFTLY on my heart it falleth,
　　Like the dew upon a flower;
Gently to my soul it calleth,
　　Yet with voice of sweetest power:
Go, be star-like; *live* the thought
That thy spirit now hath caught.

And whilst thou the thought art living,
　　Strive to work it into sound;
So, perchance, thou may'st be giving
　　Spirits in the world around,
What the stars now give to thee,
Yearnings not *to seem*, but *be!*

Than the stars what smaller seemeth ?
  Can each little point of light,
Which within the heavens gleameth,
  Blessing us with its dear sight;
Can each be a wondrous sun,
Like the one we call our own ?

Even so; and yet this teaching
  Ne'er was whispered by a star;
Never they by overreaching
  Strive to tell us what they are.
Content *to be,* they nightly gleam,
Caring little what they seem.

They have seen our wistful gazing,
  And our strange conjectures heard;
They have borne our poet-praising,
  In each diminutive word

From " Twinkle, twinkle, *little* star,
How I wonder what you are !"

To Browning's " golden arteries,"
    And Milton's " gems of heaven ;"
They've heard, too, grand discoveries,
    Often made by wisest men ;
Yet, unmoved, they nightly gleam,
Caring little what they seem.

Go, be star-like ; ever gleaming
    In the sphere God gives to thee ;
Never thinking of thy seeming
    Simply striving but *to be*.
What thou " thinkest in *thy heart*,"
What thou art to God, *thou art !*

A VOICE FROM THE STARS.

I WAS in a sober mood,
   When thought widely ranges;
I thought of evil and of good,
   I thought upon *life's changes.*

I looked upward to the stars;
   Said I, rather sadly,
No such change your quiet mars,
   Shining ever gladly.

Ye are constant, ye are true,
   We are changing ever;
Each day addeth something new,
   Something old-to sever.

Homes and friends, however dear,
　　Are both left and leaving;
What to-day is for good cheer,
　　Next day is for grieving.

Mother, sitting by the bed,
　　Smiles at her child's sleeping;
Next day, and the babe is *dead!*
　　Mother, she is weeping!

Ye are quiet, changeless, true;
　　We are changing ever;
Each day addeth something new,
　　Something old to sever.

The planet-stars made answer, softly, thus:
"Quiet, but not *changeless*, as you deem us;
Ay, *quiet*, for our changing is *God's will.*
Quiet, because 'our strength is to sit still;'

Yet as we quietly but daily turn,

Our *lights* cease not the while to *shine* and *burn*.

This also note: throughout this constant change

We do not carelessly or lightly range;

But heedful we, that as each day is done,

To have *pressed onward*, NEARER TO THE SUN!"

A STARRY WHISPER.

WHILE sitting in the shadowy twilight
   A mournful murmur floated round me,
As twilight softly deepened into night,
   The stars who heard it, answered gently.
Whether from my own heart the sound arose,
Or by the breeze was borne to me—who knows?

The way is long. I am already weary;
   And it is growing dark; and I am cold.
Oh! must my pathway always be thus dreary?
   Growing still darker until I am old?

Ah! when I started in the early morning,
   The sun was shining beautiful and bright;

Sweet flowers my every footstep were adorning,
　　Blessing me with their fragrance and their light.

But now the sun is slowly, surely sinking;
　　My flowers are closing; one by one they die.
And in this dimness, I am sad from thinking
　　What heavy darkness soon will round me lie.

And I must travel onward in the midnight,
　　So weary, and so chilled, and so alone,
And so afraid; while ever in their fearful might,
　　Will rise those yearnings I have ever known.

God help me! for the way seems long and dreary,
　　I do not love the lonely and the dark.
Of sunshine and of flowers I never weary.
　　What voice is that? a gentle whisper, hark!

　　Onward, onward, onward go!
　　Though thy sun is sinking low:

Though thy flowers *all* shall die,

Onward, God will hear thy cry;

Onward, though it be alone,

Though the way is all unknown.

Onward, though the weariness

Doth thy fainting spirit press;

Onward through the midnight gloom,

That will close around thee soon.

Onward, 'tis but twilight now,

Darker shades will cloud thy brow;

Deeper gloom o'erspread thy sky,

Then thou'lt know God hears thy cry.

First the sunlight He doth give,

In which joyously ye live;

But when this light wanes away,

When the night succeeds the day,

When the twilight ray hath gone,

And ye think ye are forlorn,

3

Look up! we will come to bless
Midnight, with our loveliness.
Ye can not see us in the day,
Not while gleams one sunny ray ;
Nor while twilight lingers near.
Darker must the sky appear.
But when comes the deep, still night,
Then will shine our starry light.
Catch from us this golden spark,
Stars shine only in the dark !

Remember, when thy day is done,
When God takes away thy sun,
It is to give thee other light,
So, *thy midnight shall be bright.*

FALLEN STAR.

"My soul kept up too much light
    Under my eyelids for the night,"

for it was the time for high and mystical revealings;
the hour which, beyond all others, possesses a mysterious yet mighty influence over the waking soul,
"the middle watch of a summer night."

No other hour of any season can rival this. Its
serene yet intense beauty, its chastened glory, its
deep, musical silence, is unequaled.

Speak not of the joys of winter evenings, in com-
parison with those of radiant, glorious, yet tranquil
summer. Bright, soft, warm; glowing with light,
fragrance, melody, and beauty, Summer, I have

no words with which to praise thee, nor the God
who gave so rich a blessing as a clear, calm, summer night!

All was still.   I stole to the opened window, and
gazed until my soul was "steeped in beauty." So
still, that it seemed as if heaven might be slumber-
ing too, and the nightly miracle of stars were the
dreams of the sleeping angels. I gazed until the
strange, deep spell the moonlight ever weaves, en-
tranced me; until I grew bewildered, as it were,
and tried in vain to draw a line of distinction between the actual and the ideal—between illusions
and reality.

All was one grand mystery. What in the day-
light we call real and practical, shrunk into insig-
nificance; while nothing seemed more tangible,
nearer to *Truth*, than those very dreams, which,

like the Yuca Filamentosa, appear so exceedingly shabby by sunlight, but when touched by the moon's softer rays, become beautiful.

Mystery! mystery! Moonlight said it; starlight breathed it; the very silence uttered it; my own soul echoed it. What was *I?* What rank did I hold in the scale of universal being?

What pure intelligences were above me?

How closely was I allied to the animals that grazed the earth? How nearly to the angelic race who worship the Holy One in perfect purity?

Mystery! mystery! Were it not for that one great truth to which the soul clings so intensely— *there is a God*—it would soon reel and stagger into insanity. It is the soul's axis; around this it re-volves in perfect security.

To one who denies the existence of the everlasting God, or who doubts his greatness, glory, power, or *goodness*, I would say: "Lift up your eyes on high, and behold who hath created these things; that bringeth out their host by number. He calleth them all by names: by the greatness of his might, for that He is strong in power, not one faileth."

I would bid him keep an unbroken watch, when the "earth is dark, but the heavens are bright," and surely before the dawn of the morning light he would be "lost in wonders so sublime," that he would exclaim: "Great things doth He, which we can not comprehend. Thine, O Lord! is the greatness, and the glory, and the majesty; for all that is in heaven and earth is thine. Thou art great, and doest wondrous things. Thou art God alone. Let all the earth fear the Lord, let all the inhabitants of the world stand in awe of him."

In the midst of my dim and dreamy musing, a star fell suddenly. I traced it. Soon it lay quivering and sparkling on a flower-bed, in my garden. I was by it in a moment; but what was my astonishment to see it gradually assume the form of a being like myself, only no larger in its dimensions than a child's little finger; yet it was perfect, and most beautiful. Dewy eyes, and hair of star-beams, pearl-white teeth, vermilion lips, and pale, rose-tinted cheeks. Her raiment was of that transparent white, as if woven of spray from a fountain. With buoyant steps she sprung from flower to flower, rejoicing in the first flush of her young and beautiful life. I watched her revel in her mirthfulness for a long time, and wondered if the tiny creature would never weary. Presently I saw her footsteps flag and her cheek pale, but her countenance was still radiant with happiness as she sought a dew-drop for a cushion. It broke beneath her weight! She appeared surprised, but, nothing daunted, she turned towards the tulip, and looked up at it appealingly; but the flower refused to lower its golden head an inch, and Fallen Star could not climb so high. With a look of singular grief and disappointment, she seated herself upon a spire of grass, the bright, green blade was delighted with its burden, but Fallen Star soon found that it was too weak for her support. More grieved and weary still, she saw a caterpillar slowly walking in its sleep; so Fallen Star thought that its fine yellow hair would form a comfortable seat, and she could have a pleasant ride, but the caterpillar shook her off indignantly.

Poor Fallen Star! what was she to do? So weary and so weak, where was she to rest? Was this the life that she had so longed for? Did all the dwellers upon earth so soon grow weary, and yearn so for a rest that they could not find? But ah! there is a violet—the world's sweetest flower—blossoming in sunshine or in shade. The first to welcome us, the last to leave us. I have had them linger in their beauty, I have gathered them from my garden on the last day of Autumn, when all else lay withered. If I have a favorite flower, it is the Violet. It has ever been to me a tender, beautiful, and faithful friend. And would the gentle violet refuse a shelter to poor little Fallen Star?

Never! So Fallen Star crept timidly amid its green leaves, and up into the fragrant flower-cup, until it nestled in the very heart of the lovely and gracious violet. Then how she trembled with delight! How the color came to her pale cheeks!

Oh! what a deep, sweet rest was hers. And I left her lying there, with her lips parted in a smile of exquisite joy, her tiny form quivering with the intense rapture of loving and being loved; of having found a home in a strong, pure, loving heart.

Yes, I left little Fallen Star to rest.

Presently I came again. I could not stay long from such beauty; but oh! what a change! The violet had perished suddenly. I raised its drooping head most tenderly; it was quite dead; no effort could revive it. The first thrill of anguish, the first violent emotion of grief with little Fallen Star was over, yet she was greatly changed. She was mute and pale; the restless joyfulness of her early life had passed away. Still she wore no look of weariness and disappointment, such as I thought to see. I remembered, too, that when I first beheld her, her

gaze was earthward only. Now, her eyes were
raised almost constantly to the place from whence
she had fallen, with a look of earnest hope and trust;
there was an unutterable yearning in her gaze, yet
it did not destroy the serenity of her sweet face;
her lips were serious, but her eyes seemed to smile
from the overflowing of peace in her heart.

Little Fallen Star did not play any more. She
did not twist together the blades of grass, or scatter
the pollen from the anthers, as I saw her do in her
first glad frolics, nor did she sit down in mournful
idleness; but patiently her little fingers gathered
the seeds that had ripened, and were just ready to
fall, and scattered them where no seed had been
sown; she raised, and bound up the blades of grass
that had been trodden under foot and bruised in
the day time; and where a flower was overburdened

with dew, she would relieve it by carrying the precious drops to some tiny blossoms that were overshadowed by larger plants, and were parched, and thirsting for the refreshing moisture.

It was thus that little Fallen Star passed the remainder of the night. But when " the earth at day-dawn lifted up her head out of her sleep, star-watched, to face the sun," a starry brilliant, glimmering in the blue above, showed that Fallen Star had returned to her home on high; but the memory of the truth she murmured as she left us, the great and beautiful truth that she had learned during her earthly pilgrimage, may bring a blessing to many a weary heart, and aching soul:

"TO BLESS, IS TO BE BLEST."